Katie Kazoo, SWITCHEROO

Major League Mess-Up

by Nancy Krulik • illustrated by John & Wendy

Grosset & Dunlap

For my parents, Gladys and Steve, baseball
fans since the Ebbets Field days!—N.K.

For Sarah, a most valuable player: We're glad
we're on her team!—J&W

GROSSET & DUNLAP
Published by the Penguin Group
Penguin Group (USA) Inc., 375 Hudson Street, New York, New York 10014, USA
Penguin Group (Canada), 90 Eglinton Avenue East, Suite 700, Toronto,
Ontario M4P 2Y3, Canada
(a division of Pearson Penguin Canada Inc.)
Penguin Books Ltd., 80 Strand, London WC2R 0RL, England
Penguin Group Ireland, 25 St. Stephen's Green, Dublin 2, Ireland
(a division of Penguin Books Ltd.)
Penguin Group (Australia), 250 Camberwell Road, Camberwell,
Victoria 3124, Australia
(a division of Pearson Australia Group Pty. Ltd.)
Penguin Books India Pvt. Ltd., 11 Community Centre, Panchsheel Park,
New Delhi—110 017, India
Penguin Group (NZ), 67 Apollo Drive, Rosedale, North Shore 0632, New Zealand
(a division of Pearson New Zealand Ltd.)
Penguin Books (South Africa) (Pty.) Ltd., 24 Sturdee Avenue,
Rosebank, Johannesburg 2196, South Africa

Penguin Books Ltd., Registered Offices: 80 Strand, London WC2R 0RL, England

Text copyright © 2008 by Nancy Krulik. Illustrations copyright © 2008
by John and Wendy. All rights reserved. Published by Grosset & Dunlap, a
division of Penguin Young Readers Group, 345 Hudson Street, New York, New
York 10014. GROSSET & DUNLAP is a trademark of Penguin Group (USA) Inc.
Printed in the U.S.A.

Library of Congress Control Number: 2007039736

ISBN 978-0-448-44676-9   10 9 8 7

Chapter 1

"Take me out to the ball game! Take me out with the crowd," Katie Carew sang out with her dad and her friends during the seventh inning stretch. At the end of the song, she plopped down in the hard blue seat at Cherrydale Stadium right between her two best friends, Suzanne Lock and Jeremy Fox. "I love baseball games," she told them.

"Me too!" Jeremy exclaimed. "Especially when the Cherrydale Porcupines are on a winning streak."

"The Porcupines are really *sticking* it to the competition," Katie agreed. She pointed to the hat she was wearing. It was a baseball cap with blue and green rubber porcupine spikes all over.

"I can't believe you are wearing that thing on your head," Suzanne said. "It's hideous."

"No it's not," Katie insisted. "It shows I have team spirit."

"We've got that spirit," Jeremy cheered.

"Come on, let's hear it!" Katie echoed.

"Go Porcupines!" Suzanne and Jeremy shouted.

"A little louder," Katie's dad sang out, joining in on their cheer.

"GO PORCUPINES!" the kids screamed.

Katie's father laughed. "Say it loud. Say it proud!" he cheered.

Katie smiled. They were definitely loud. But not nearly as loud as the guy in the green and blue striped shirt selling popcorn.

"Popcorn! Get your popcorn here!" he called out.

"Are you kids hungry?" Mr. Carew asked Jeremy, Suzanne, and Katie.

"I'd like some popcorn, please," Suzanne said.

"Me too," Jeremy agreed.

"Make it three," Katie chimed in.

As Mr. Carew paid the man for the three cartons of popcorn, Jeremy looked down at the baseball field. "We can see every player perfectly from here," he said.

"I always get seats near first base," Katie's dad told him. "It's where *my* dad and I sat when I was a teenager."

Katie giggled. It was kind of hard to imagine her grown-up dad as a teenage boy.

"Did you really go to college with Jim Borden, the old shortstop?" Jeremy asked Mr. Carew. "Katie told us you did."

Katie's dad nodded. "He was a couple of years ahead of me in school, but I saw him around campus. He was amazing back then. He didn't hit anything but home runs!"

"Just like Mike Reed now," Jeremy said.

Katie frowned. Mike Reed was the Porcupines' new starting shortstop. Because of him, her favorite player, Jim Borden, had

to sit on the bench.

"I think Jim Borden should *still* be the starting shortstop!" Katie exclaimed.

"He can't play as well as he used to. This is probably his last season," Katie's dad explained. "Age catches up with athletes—even the great ones."

"But you are always saying how important experience is. And Jim Borden has plenty of that," Katie reminded her father. Then she turned to Jeremy. "And besides, he's so nice. Remember back in second grade when he came to school on career day? He talked about being a baseball player. At recess, he even showed us how to catch fly balls. And helped us with our batting, too. You should be more loyal, Jeremy."

"Jim Borden was a nice guy, but Mike Reed is going to take us to the championships," Jeremy insisted. "Do you know how many home runs he's hit this season?"

"Do you like Jim Borden better than Mike Reed?" Katie asked Suzanne.

Suzanne just shrugged. "I don't care who plays," she said. "I'm just here because it gave me an excuse to wear my green and blue glitter shirt."

Katie rolled her eyes. "Well, I care!" she insisted. "Jim Borden is a much better player than Mike Reed."

"You wish," Jeremy told her.

Katie's face turned beet-red. "I do not!" she shouted angrily. "I do not wish anything!"

Mr. Carew, Jeremy, and Suzanne all looked at Katie as though she were nuts.

But Katie wasn't nuts. Not at all. She just hated wishes.

Chapter 2

Katie had learned all about wishes last year, when she was in third grade. It started one terrible, horrible day when Katie had missed the football and lost the game for her team. Then she'd fallen in a big mud puddle and ruined her favorite pair of jeans. Even worse, she'd let out a huge embarrassing burp in front of the whole class.

That night, Katie had wished she could be anyone but herself. There must have been a shooting star overhead or something, because the next day the magic wind came.

The magic wind was a superstrong, tornado-like wind that blew only around Katie. It was so powerful that every time it came, it turned Katie into someone else.

The first time the magic wind came it turned Katie into Speedy, the class 3A hamster. She'd been stuck in Speedy's cage all morning with nothing to do but run around and around on his hamster wheel and eat wooden chew sticks. When she had finally escaped she wound up hidden inside George Brennan's stinky sneaker! Yuck!

Katie was so glad when the magic wind returned and changed her back into herself. But that wasn't the end of it. The magic wind kept coming back.

One time it turned her into Suzanne right before a big fashion show. What a disaster that had been! Katie had no idea how to model. She put on Suzanne's outfit backward and almost fell off the runway.

Poor Suzanne. Her first fashion show had been a disaster. And she had no idea how or why that had happened.

That was the biggest problem with the magic wind. It always blew in trouble for the person Katie turned into. Then it was up to Katie to make things right again.

Like the time the magic wind switcherooed Katie into her dentist, Dr. Sang. When little Matthew Weber walked into the office, she squirted him with water and scared him so much that he refused to ever go to the dentist again.

The magic wind was the reason Katie didn't make wishes anymore. She knew how bad things could be if they came true.

But of course, she couldn't tell her dad or her friends that. They wouldn't believe her if she did. Katie wouldn't believe it herself—if it didn't keep happening to her.

Still, she had to say *something*.

"I . . . um . . . I just meant that Jim Borden's a really talented shortstop," Katie told them. "It's not fair to put someone on the bench just because someone new joined the team."

"Hey, you guys, Mike Reed's up at bat," Suzanne interrupted.

They all looked down onto the field.

Mike Reed pulled the bat back over his right shoulder, and jutted his backside out. Then he glared in the pitcher's direction. It was like he was daring the pitcher to throw a really good one.

The pitcher wound up. The ball zoomed through the air and . . .

Crack. The sound of the ball hitting Mike Reed's bat was really loud. Katie watched as the ball soared up in the air. It moved farther and farther away. Finally it landed in the stands, right behind center field.

"Another home run for Mike Reed!" the stadium announcer shouted.

The crowd leaped to its feet and began to cheer. The words REED ROCKS! flashed across the giant jumbotron screen above left field.

Katie sighed. Poor Jim Borden. It looked like he'd be warming the bench for a while.

Chapter 3

"Boy, that was an exciting game!" Jeremy said as he got out of the car in front of Katie's house.

Katie didn't say anything. She was really happy that the Porcupines had won. It just would have been nice to see Jim Borden play.

Just then, Katie's next-door neighbor, Mrs. Derkman, looked up from her gardening. "Hey," she called out to the kids. "Did the Porcupines win?"

"Oh yeah!" Jeremy cheered.

Mrs. Derkman raised her fist high. "Go Porcupines!" she cheered.

"It stinks to go to a game if your team loses," Suzanne said.

"Every team loses sometime, Suzanne," Mrs. Derkman reminded her. "You have to learn how to win and lose gracefully."

Suzanne rolled her eyes at Katie. Katie knew just what her friend was thinking. She, Jeremy, and Suzanne had all had Mrs. Derkman as a teacher in third grade. Mrs. Derkman's problem was she couldn't stop being a teacher, even when she wasn't in school.

"Your roses are looking spectacular, Barbara," Katie's dad said to Mrs. Derkman.

"Thanks, Dave," Mrs. Derkman replied. "I'm entering them in the garden club competition next weekend."

"I think you have a good shot at getting a ribbon," Katie's dad told her.

Katie walked over and sniffed at one of the ruby-red blossoms. "Oooh! They smell so nice."

"I love flowers." Suzanne reached out to touch one of the blossoms.

"Suzanne! Don't touch my babies," Mrs. Derkman exclaimed.

Katie looked at Mrs. Derkman strangely. Sometimes the things her third-grade teacher said totally surprised her. "Your *babies*?"

"Well, I've raised these rosebushes ever since they were seedlings," Mrs. Derkman explained. "I've fed them, watered them, and taken care of them. So they're kind of like my babies. You understand?"

Katie didn't. But she kept quiet. It was easier that way.

Suzanne didn't keep quiet, though. "What do you feed your babies?" she asked.

Mrs. Derkman raised the brim of her big white hat and wiped a little sweat from her brow. "I have a special plant food that's made just for roses," she told Suzanne. "And I make sure to plant my roses in special dirt that has a lot of healthy minerals in it."

Katie wrinkled her nose. Special dirt? Wasn't dirt just dirt?

"How do you get the roses to grow so big?" Suzanne asked.

"Well, for starters, I cut away any dead branches," Mrs. Derkman said, holding up a big pair of garden scissors. "That makes the plant healthier. And I make sure that all my rosebushes are planted in a spot that gets at least six hours of sunlight a day."

"Wow, that's so interesting," Suzanne said.

"She's got to be kidding," Jeremy whispered to Katie.

But Suzanne wasn't kidding. She seemed to hang on everything Mrs. Derkman was saying. She watched carefully as Mrs. Derkman showed her how to cut a dying branch from one of the bushes.

"That's called pruning," Mrs. Derkman told Suzanne.

Katie sighed. She was getting really bored. "Um . . . Suzanne," she said, finally. "Weren't you, Jeremy, and I going to play catch in my backyard?"

Suzanne frowned. "Well, I kind of wanted to help Mrs. Derkman with the . . ." she began.

Bzzzzz . . . Just then a bee began buzzing near Mrs. Derkman's face.

"AAAAHHHHH!" the teacher cried out. "A bee! I hate bees!"

Katie bit her lip and tried not to giggle. Mrs. Derkman hated all kinds of bugs, not just bees.

Mrs. Derkman leaped up and began running around the yard, waving her hands wildly in front of her. "Get away from me!" she shouted to the bee.

Katie knew yelling at the bee wouldn't help. Bees don't understand English!

But Mrs. Derkman kept yelling and yelling. "Get out of here! Shoo!" she screamed.

Since the bee wouldn't leave, Mrs. Derkman did. She darted into her house and slammed the door shut—leaving the buzzing bee outside.

As soon as Mrs. Derkman was inside, Katie and Jeremy both started laughing.

"She's so funny when bugs get near her," Jeremy said. He waved his arms in the air and ran around in a circle like Mrs. Derkman was doing.

Katie giggled harder—until her father shot her a look.

Oops. "Jeremy, let's go play ball," Katie said, trying to change the subject.

"Okay," Jeremy agreed.

"Are you coming, Suzanne?" Katie asked.

"Yeah, sure!" she agreed.

"Wait until you guys see my fastball," Jeremy boasted. "It stings harder than any bee."

"You know what else stings harder than a bee?" Katie asked.

"What?" Suzanne wondered.

"A Porcupine!" Katie cheered. "The Porcupines are mighty fine!"

"They are *now*," Jeremy agreed. "Thanks to Mike Reed. Reed's got speed!"

"Yeah! Reed's got speed!" Suzanne chimed in.

Katie tried to come up with a cheer for Jim Borden. But nothing rhymed with Borden. And besides, Jim hadn't done much to cheer about lately.

He hadn't done much of anything, besides warm the bench.

Grrr.

Chapter 4

The next morning, when Katie arrived at school, everyone was talking about the Cherrydale Porcupines.

"We're gonna go all the way this year," Kadeem Carter said.

"The world champion Cherrydale Porcupines. I like the sound of that," George Brennan agreed.

Katie stared at the boys in amazement. George and Kadeem never agreed on anything.

"Mike Reed is the most incredible player in the history of the world," Mandy Banks chimed in. "Did you see those home runs he hit?"

"Of course," Jeremy told her. "I was at the game with Katie and Suzanne."

"Lucky you," Mandy said, turning to Katie. "You got to see Mike Reed knock in those runs."

"Don't you guys care about Jim Borden anymore? He's the one who came to our school, not Mike Reed!" she reminded her friends.

"That was back when you were in second grade. I didn't even go to this school then," George reminded her. Then he turned back to Kadeem. "Do you think Reed could be the league's most valuable player this year?" he asked.

Before Kadeem could answer, Suzanne came bounding onto the playground. She leaped right into the middle of the conversation. "Do you like my dress?" she asked Katie and Mandy, totally ignoring the boys.

Usually it annoyed Katie when Suzanne tried to make herself the center of attention. But today she was glad. She was tired of hearing about wonderful, fabulous, amazing Mike Reed. Still, she wasn't sure how to answer

Suzanne's question. The dress was green with red roses all over it. Suzanne kind of looked like a rosebush with hair.

But of course, Katie could never say that. So instead, she just said, "It's . . . um . . . really flowery."

"Yeah," Mandy agreed. "It sure has a lot of roses on it."

"I know," Suzanne said. "When I saw it at the mall last night I knew I just had to have it."

Just then, George began to twirl around. "How do you guys like my outfit?" he asked in a high, squeaky voice.

"Oh, it's just divine," Jeremy replied, trying to sound like a girl, too. "You have such adorable clothes."

"Don't I?" George agreed. The boys all began to laugh.

Suzanne rolled her eyes. "You are such children!" she shouted at them.

"Yeah, we are," Jeremy agreed.

"So are you," George reminded her.

Suzanne rolled her eyes again, but she didn't say anything else.

"So do you guys want to play ball after school today?" Jeremy asked, changing the subject back to baseball again. "We can go to my house."

"Sure," Kadeem agreed. "We'll get Kevin to play, too."

"How about you, Katie Kazoo?" George asked Katie, using the way-cool nickname he'd given her back in third grade.

"I'll play," Katie agreed. "And I think Emma W. is free after school today, too."

"Me too," Mandy said. "How about you Suzanne?"

Suzanne thought for a minute. "I kind of have something else to do today," she told the kids. "Something much more important."

"More important than baseball?" Jeremy asked her.

"Impossible," Kadeem added.

George shrugged. He and Suzanne weren't

friends—at all. Katie could tell he didn't care if she played with them or not. Besides, George had that look on his face—the one he got when he was about to tell a joke!

"Hey, do you guys know what it's called when a pig hits a ball over a fence?" he asked the kids.

"What?" Mandy asked him.

"A ham run!" George replied. He laughed really hard.

So did everyone else—except Kadeem. He told his own joke instead.

"When is a base runner like an electric light?" he asked the kids.

"When?" Jeremy asked him.

"When they're both out," Kadeem told him.

The kids all laughed again. Except George. He wasn't about to let Kadeem get the last laugh.

"What has six arms, six legs, and catches flies?" George asked the kids.

"What?" Mandy wondered.

"A baseball team outfield!" George exclaimed.

Katie grinned. She loved when George and Kadeem had one of their joke-offs. And this time it was a baseball joke-off. Every joke was a home run!

Chapter 5

"You're a pretty good pitcher," George complimented Jeremy the next morning as the kids gathered on the playground before school.

"You're not a bad hitter," Jeremy complimented George back. "Although I don't think my mom was too happy when you knocked down the bird feeder."

George shrugged and lifted his blue and green prickly Porcupines hat. "Sorry," he apologized.

"That was actually my fault," Katie admitted. "I should have caught that ball."

"It's okay," Jeremy told her. "Not everyone can play shortstop like Mike Reed."

Katie opened her mouth to say something, but stopped suddenly. Suzanne had just walked onto the playground. The sight of her made Katie speechless.

"Oh my goodness," Emma W. exclaimed.

"What is she wearing?" Kadeem asked.

"Suzanne just gets weirder and weirder," George said.

Ordinarily, Katie would have scolded George for making fun of Suzanne. But she couldn't this time. Suzanne did look . . . well, *different* was one way of putting it.

Suzanne thought of herself as the fashion expert of the fourth grade. But right now, Suzanne looked anything *but* fashionable. She was wearing a pair of blue faded overalls and a huge straw hat. There was nothing glitzy or glamorous about her.

If Suzanne noticed that all the kids were staring at her, she didn't show it. She just smiled. "Hi guys," she greeted them. "How did the baseball game go?"

"Uh . . . fine," Mandy said.

"Yeah," Emma W. agreed. "So, how was your afternoon?"

From under the wide brim of her hat Suzanne said, "Great. I had a blast."

"Where'd you get that hat?" Kadeem asked her.

"Mrs. Derkman gave it to me," Suzanne said. "Do you like it?"

"I think it's weird," George told her.

Suzanne looked at the blue and green Porcupines cap on George's head. "You should talk," she told him.

"Why did Mrs. Derkman give you a hat?" Katie asked Suzanne.

"Because the sun was in my eyes yesterday while we were in her garden," Suzanne told her.

So *that* was the big important thing Suzanne had to do after school.

"You spent the afternoon with Mrs. Derkman?" Katie sounded amazed.

Suzanne nodded. "It was so much fun. Mrs.

Derkman even let me spread mulch out around the plants."

"Spread the *what*?" Mandy asked.

"Mulch," Suzanne repeated. "Mrs. Derkman uses wood chips. But you can spread hay or grass clippings around the plants, too. Mulch keeps the moisture in the soil. But wood chips are pretty. That's why Mrs. Derkman puts them around her babies."

"Her what?" Emma W. asked.

"That's what she calls her roses," Suzanne explained. "She's so protective. Even Snowball isn't allowed near her babies."

Katie already knew that. Snowball was Mrs. Derkman's dog, and Katie's cocker spaniel Pepper's best friend. Any time Snowball or Pepper went near the rosebushes, Mrs. Derkman had a fit.

"But she let *me* help with the roses," Suzanne boasted. "Mrs. Derkman says I have a green thumb."

George stared at Suzanne's hand. "It looks

plain old skin color to me," he told her.

Suzanne ignored George. "That means I have a talent for gardening," Suzanne went on. "Mrs. Derkman even asked me to come to her house on Saturday. That's when the garden club will be judging her roses."

"Saturday?" Jeremy and Katie said at once.

"But we're supposed to go to the game," Katie told her.

"It was all arranged with my Aunt Sheila," Jeremy added.

"Oh, I'm sure you can get someone to take my place," Suzanne told Katie and Jeremy.

Katie looked at her friends. She could tell both Kadeem and George hoped Jeremy would ask them to go.

"Man, I would really love to see Mike Reed in person," George said.

"So would I," Kadeem told him. "I'm Reed's biggest fan."

"No way," George said. "I am."

"Mike Reed! Mike Reed!" Kadeem chanted.

"Mike Reed! Mike Reed!" George shouted louder.

"Mike REED!" Kadeem screamed.

Katie sighed. This was getting ridiculous.

Almost as ridiculous as Suzanne's big straw hat!

Chapter 6

"Get away from those babies!"

Katie jumped at the sound of a screaming voice. She had spent the afternoon at Emma W.'s and was cutting across Mrs. Derkman's yard so she wouldn't be late for dinner. Mrs. Derkman hated people walking on her lawn.

Katie looked around. Funny . . . there didn't seem to be anyone in the Derkmans' yard. Boy, teachers really had supervision!

"I'm sorry, Mrs. Derkman," Katie called out once she was back on the sidewalk.

But it wasn't Mrs. Derkman who had been shouting at Katie. It was Suzanne. At least Katie *thought* it was Suzanne who leaped out from behind a drainpipe. It was hard to tell who it was. The big-brimmed straw hat was hiding most of her face.

"What are you doing?" Katie asked her.

"Standing guard," Suzanne told her. "So no one can attack."

"Attack what?" Katie wondered.

"The roses," Suzanne answered.

"Who would want to do that?"

"Mrs. Derkman told me those garden club women will do anything to win," Suzanne explained. "So I promised to watch our babies until I had to go home for supper."

"*Our* babies?" Katie repeated.

Suzanne nodded. "Mrs. Derkman said I'm almost like a second mom to them. I have to protect them from our enemies."

Katie laughed. "Suzanne, you make it sound like this garden club contest is a war," she said.

"It is," Suzanne replied. "The War of the Roses."

* * *

The next day, Katie spotted George Brennan on the playground. He was hard to miss in his bright green and blue T-shirt and blue and green rubber Porcupines cap. Just in case someone couldn't guess he was a Porcupines fan, he was carrying a green and blue "We're number one" foam finger.

"Guess who Jeremy picked to go to the game on Saturday," George said.

Katie giggled. "Um . . . you?" she teased.

"Oh yeah!" George cheered. "I'm so psyched. I can almost taste those hot dogs, and the soda, and, of course, the Cracker Jacks. You can't go to a ball game and not eat Cracker Jacks!"

"Are you planning to watch the game between bites?" Katie asked him.

"Definitely," George said. "I won't miss a single move Mike Reed makes!"

Katie frowned. "You know, he's not the only person on the team. There are lots of players who have made the Porcupines who they are!" she insisted. "Like Jim Borden, for instance. He's definitely heading for the Hall of Fame!"

But George didn't seem to care. "Gee, do you think Mike Reed eats Cracker Jacks?" he asked Katie. "Nah. He's probably more of a cotton candy kind of guy."

Katie sighed. "Oh what's the point?" she grumbled as she walked away.

Chapter 7

At the game on Saturday, Katie had on her blue jeans, her cool new turquoise sneakers, and her old Jim Borden jersey.

Jeremy and George were wearing jerseys, too—Mike Reed jerseys.

So was Jeremy's Aunt Sheila.

And the big man in the row in front of Katie.

Not to mention the whole family eating hot dogs and chips in the boxed seats behind first base.

And the teenage boy buying Cracker Jacks from the vendor on the steps.

"Come on, you guys, let's go down toward the field," Jeremy said to Katie and George.

"Yeah," George agreed. "I brought a baseball for the players to sign."

"Cool," Jeremy said. He was holding a black marker. "I hope Mike Reed will sign my jersey."

"How about you, Katie?" George asked.

"I'm going to ask Jim Borden to sign mine," she said.

"Hurry up then," Jeremy told her as they ran down the stairs toward the Porcupines' dugout. "It's just a few minutes till the game starts."

"Who knows if Jim Borden will even be here?" George said. "I mean, the coach isn't going to play him with Mike Reed on the team."

"Mike Reed's not so great," Katie told George. "I've seen him make a whole bunch of errors in the field. And the homers? Well, maybe he's just on a lucky streak."

George and Jeremy stared at her for a minute. Neither one of them said a word.

"What?" Katie asked them.

"Um . . . Katie," George said slowly. He

pointed behind her.

Katie turned around. There was Mike Reed, two feet away. He looked huge. And his big bushy mustache was twitching. "I just try to do my best every game," he told Katie. He sounded more upset than angry. "That's all any ball player can do." He turned and walked back into the dugout.

Oops. Now Katie felt really bad. She hadn't meant to hurt anyone's feelings. She was just trying to defend *her* favorite shortstop.

But she *had* hurt Mike Reed's feelings. A bunch of fans nearby didn't look too happy, either.

"What's your problem?" one man shouted at Katie.

"Are you trying to jinx Mike?" a girl asked her.

Katie could feel her cheeks getting all hot and red. Tears were starting to form in her eyes. She was *sooo* embarrassed.

So she did what any fourth-grade girl would

do in the same situation. She ran back toward
her seat as fast as she could. She darted up the
stairs, past the food stands and the cart selling
blue and green Porcupines hats and "I Like
Mike" banners.

Just then, Katie spotted a small door behind
one of the ice cream stands. *Maybe it's a*

bathroom or something, she thought.

Actually it didn't really matter to Katie what was behind that door—as long as she got away from all those angry fans in their Mike Reed shirts.

Quickly, Katie turned the knob and found herself all alone in a little room. Well, all alone except for lots of mops, buckets, sponges, and plastic bags. Katie had wound up inside the janitor's closet.

It kind of smelled in there. But Katie didn't mind. She was happy to just be by herself for a few minutes so she could take a deep breath. Well, not *too* deep.

Just then, Katie felt a cool breeze blowing on the back of her neck. That was weird. There weren't any windows in the janitor's closet. And the door was shut tight. So where was the breeze coming from?

Katie didn't have time to think about that. At that moment, the breeze began blowing colder and harder, until it was like a wild tornado. A tornado that was only spinning around Katie.

Oh, no! This wasn't an ordinary wind. It was the magic wind. It had followed Katie all the way to the baseball game.

And, boy, was it blowing. The wind was so fierce, Katie was afraid it might blow her all the way to China! She shut her eyes tight and tried not to cry.

And then it stopped. Just like that. The magic wind was gone.

So was Katie Kazoo. She'd been turned into someone else. One, two, switcheroo!

The question was, who?

Chapter 8

"Yeah! Hooray! Woo-hoo! Porcupines rule!"

As soon as the wind stopped blowing in her ears, Katie heard a loud cheer. Thousands of people all screaming at once. The noise scared her.

Katie gulped. Where had the wind blown her this time?

Slowly, she opened her eyes and looked around. Yikes! She was running from the dugout to the infield. The screaming was coming from the crowd in the stands.

Katie squinted into the sun. The people in the stands looked really small and crunched together. Kind of like a sea of green and blue ants.

Green and blue. The colors Porcupines fans wore.

She looked down at herself. She was wearing green and blue stripes, too. Her way-cool turquoise sneakers were gone. Instead she was wearing ugly black cleats.

She reached up and touched the top of her head. She was still wearing a baseball hat. But this hat wasn't rubber and prickly. It was made of cloth—*a real baseball player's hat.*

Well, one thing was for sure. Katie was a Porcupine. The questions was, which one?

Suddenly Katie had a really bad feeling. Even playing against fourth graders, she wasn't that great at baseball. How was she going to hit a ball that was thrown by a real pitcher?

Katie took a deep breath and tried to calm down. Maybe she wasn't actually a Porcupines *player.* Maybe she was someone else. Like the batboy or something. That wouldn't be so bad. The batboy didn't have to do much. He just picked up foul balls and handed the players their bats. She could handle that.

Boy, it was really hot out. Katie wiped some sweat from under her nose. Her hand brushed against a bush of thick, bristly hair.

She made a face. Oooh, gross. Katie had a mustache.

The crowd began to laugh.

Katie wondered what was so funny.

Just then some music began to play. "CHARGE!" the crowd shouted out.

Whoa! The shouting was so loud it scared Katie. She jumped.

The crowd laughed harder.

As Katie turned around to see what was so funny, she spotted the big jumbotron above left field. Mike Reed was on the screen.

Katie frowned. Even here she couldn't get away from him.

Uh-oh. Mike Reed was frowning now, too.

Katie rolled her eyes and waved her arms in the air.

Sure enough, on the jumbotron, Mike Reed

did the same thing.

Double uh-oh. Could the magic wind have turned her into a superstar shortstop—the shortstop she *hated*—just as the game was starting?

Even the magic wind couldn't be that mean . . . could it?

There was only one way to find out. She would have to do something Mike Reed would never do in front of a crowd. Not in a million years. She turned around wiggled her rear end at everybody.

"Do the Mike dance," someone shouted from the seats near first base.

They all wiggled their rear ends.

"Yo, Mike," the second baseman called out. "What are you doing, man? This is an important game. Stop clowning around."

Katie looked at the second baseman. He was staring right at her. She pointed to herself. "Who me?" she asked.

"Yeah you, Mike. What's with all the clowning? Get serious."

Katie gulped. That settled it. She wasn't the batboy. And she wasn't just any player on the Porcupines now. She was Mike Reed. Home-run king and star shortstop.

This was *sooooo* not good!

Chapter 9

It was the top of the first inning.

"Two outs, nobody on," the stadium announcer called out.

Katie smiled. So far so good. The Porcupines' pitcher had struck out the first two Apple Valley Anteaters. Katie hadn't had to do anything but stand here. Now if the pitcher could just strike out this last batter, she could go back into the dugout and figure out what to do next.

The pitcher pulled his arm back, turned slightly, and released the ball. It sped straight toward home plate. And then . . .

Crack! The sound of the baseball hitting a

bat sure sounded louder on the field than it did from the bleachers.

The ball looked like it was moving a lot faster from here, too. *Whoosh!* It was heading right for Katie. She ducked down and the ball soared over her head, missing her by just inches.

Phew. That ball could have knocked her out cold.

But the crowd was angry. Really angry. They started to boo.

Oops. She'd forgotten she was Mike Reed now. He was never afraid of the ball.

Katie punched her fist into her glove, just like the real baseball players did. *I'm Mike Reed. I'm Mike Reed,* she told herself. *So act like Mike Reed.* She thought about spitting, but that was way too gross.

Crack! The next batter hit the ball high up in the air. The ball was soaring between second and third base—right where Katie was standing.

This time Katie was ready. She held her arm way up with her glove wide-open.

"I got it, I got it!" Katie shouted as she ran to catch the ball.

"No, I've got it," the second baseman screamed.

But Katie paid no attention. She was determined not mess up this time. She just kept running.

The sun was awfully bright. She could barely see anything. Still, she kept running in the direction the ball was heading.

Smack! Katie slammed right into the second baseman.

"Oomph," she groaned as she fell to the ground. That hurt.

But what hurt worse was seeing the ball fall on the ground right between them.

"I told you I had it," the second baseman growled as he scooped up the ball and threw it toward first base. But it was too late. The runner was safe. Now there was someone on first and second.

The crowd began booing again.

All this booing was just too much for Katie to take. She felt her throat closing and her eyes prickled. The crowd was being so mean. After all, she was trying her best.

The next thing the fans saw on the jumbotron was big, strong Mike Reed, *crying like a little kid.*

✳ ✳ ✳

The Porcupines' pitcher managed to save the rest of the inning. He pitched another strike-out. The Anteaters hadn't scored a single run.

Katie hurried into the dugout and sat down on the far corner of the bench. She didn't want to talk to any of the other players.

But a tall, skinny player walked over and sat down on the bench beside her. Katie gasped. It was Jim Borden, her favorite Porcupine!

"Oh my gosh! It's so good to see you again, Jim," Katie blurted out.

Jim looked at her strangely. "Huh?" he asked.

Oops. Katie kept forgetting she was Mike Reed. "I mean it's always good to see you, Jim."

"Yeah. Back at ya," Jim said. "Anyway, I just wanted to tell you not to worry about what happened out there. Anyone can have an off day." He patted Katie on the back. "Don't let the booing get to you. You're on deck. Hit a homer, and everybody will be loving you again."

Katie gasped. On deck. That meant she was batting next.

It had been tough enough trying to be Mike Reed in the field. But now she was expected to hit a home run.

This was *soooo* not good.

Katie picked up a bat and watched the

Porcupine batter standing at the plate.

Crack . . . the batter sent the ball out into center field. He ran toward first base.

"Safe!" the umpire shouted.

The crowd began to cheer. "Mike! Mike! Mike!"

"Batter up!" the umpire shouted. He stared right at Katie.

Gulp. *That means me*, she thought.

There was no getting out of this now. She picked up the big, heavy bat and walked toward the plate.

Katie stood there, watching the pitcher as he wound up. She tried to remember everything Jim Borden had told the kids about batting when he'd visited their school.

Don't choke up on the bat.

Put most of your weight on the balls of your feet, not the heels.

Face the pitcher.

Keep your head still.

And never—*ever*—take your eyes off the ball.

Okay, that last one was tough. Because the Anteaters' pitcher threw the ball so fast, Katie couldn't even see it. She just heard it whiz past her head.

"Strike!" the umpire shouted.

Katie tried not to get rattled. She had at least two more chances to . . .

Whoosh! Another ball sped right past Katie while she was busy thinking.

"Strike two," the umpire shouted out.

"Hey!" Katie exclaimed. "I wasn't ready."

The umpire and the Anteaters' catcher gave her an odd look.

"Um . . . I mean . . . I'm ready now," Katie said, trying to sound like a tough grown-up baseball player.

The pitcher threw another fastball. This time,

Katie swung the bat. *Hard*. So hard she whirled around like a helicopter blade.

"Strike three!" the umpire shouted. "You're out!"

The crowd began booing again. They were really mad.

As she headed into the dugout, Katie kept her head down, so no one could see her tears. She walked past all the Porcupines players on the bench, and right out the door.

She didn't even stop to hear what Jim Borden was saying to her.

* * *

The loneliest place in the whole stadium right now was the players' locker room. It was the perfect place to hide from the booing crowd. Only they weren't booing now. They were cheering. That had to mean the next Porcupine player had gotten on base. Well, that was good at least.

But not good enough to make Katie feel better. She sat down on the bench and rested her head in her hands. Tears began to fall down her big manly cheeks. Lots of tears landed in her thick, bushy mustache. It was getting all wet and clumpy.

Just then, Katie felt a cool breeze on the back of her neck. Before she could even turn around to look for an open window, the breeze picked up speed. It began blowing harder and harder. In a flash, it had turned into a fierce tornado—a tornado that was only blowing around Katie.

The magic wind had returned. And it was really wild this time.

Katie shut her eyes tight. She held on to the bench and tried to keep from being blown away. The wind whipped harder and harder around her body. Faster and faster. Whirring all around.

And then it stopped. Just like that.

The magic wind was gone.

Katie Kazoo was back!

So was Mike Reed. And boy did he look confused.

Chapter 10

"What are you doing here?" Mike asked Katie. He looked around the locker room. "What am *I* doing here?" he added.

"You came in here after you struck out," Katie said quietly.

"I struck out?" Mike asked, shaking his head. "Whoa. You mean that really happened? I thought I was dreaming or something. It's all kind of fuzzy."

Katie sighed. Mike hadn't really struck out. *She* had. But she couldn't tell him that.

"Who are you, anyway?" Mike asked.

"My name's Katie Carew," Katie said, holding out her hand.

"Kids aren't allowed in the locker room," Mike told Katie. "I can give you a quick autograph and then you have to go, okay?"

"Oh, I don't want an autograph," Katie said.

"I don't blame you," Mike said. "I wouldn't want my autograph either after the way I just played."

That made Katie feel awful.

"It's not that," she assured him. "It's just that I think you should get out there. They'll think you're a bad sport if you don't."

Mike nodded. "I guess you're right. But I don't even know how to explain what happened to the coach."

"That's okay," Katie said. "I'm sure everyone will forgive you once you start hitting home runs again."

"That's just what Jim Borden told me," Mike told her.

"I know," Katie replied.

Mike looked at her strangely. "How do you know what he said to me?"

Oops. "Um . . . I just figured," Katie said quickly. "Now go out there and hit a homer!"

✴ ✴ ✴

Unfortunately, Mike *didn't* start hitting home runs again. In fact, he struck out three more times during the game that the Porcupines lost. The crowd was not happy.

"He's in such a bad slump," George said as he, Katie, and Jeremy left the ballpark at the end of the day.

"Yeah, you missed the worst part, Katie," Jeremy said. "When you were in the bathroom, Mike messed up two easy plays!"

Katie frowned. She hadn't been in the bathroom then, of course. That was just what she'd told her friends. What else could she have said? She couldn't tell them that she was the one making the errors.

"Well, it looks like you could get your wish, Katie Kazoo," George told her. "If Mike Reed is benched, Jim Borden will play."

Any other time, that would have made Katie really happy. But now it didn't. She knew this time it wasn't really fair.

* * *

George was right. That night on the news, Mike Reed spoke to a sports reporter. He told him, "I made some bad plays and I let it get to me. I have a lot to learn, especially from experienced players like Jim Borden."

Katie looked at Mike Reed's face. He looked so sad. That made Katie feel really bad.

"He's right. Jim Borden has a lot to teach the other players," Katie told her dad. "Even Mike Reed said so."

"I have always thought the Porcupines needed an infield coach," Mr. Carew agreed. "And today's game sure proves me right. Reed wasn't the only one messing up in the infield today."

"An infield coach . . ." Katie murmured. Then she smiled brightly.

Katie had just gotten one of her great ideas!

Chapter 11

On Sunday morning, Katie woke up early. She rode her bike over to the stadium. She wanted to get there while the Porcupines were practicing for their next game.

"All right, Jim," Katie heard someone shouting from the baseball field. "This one's coming right at you!"

Sure enough, a batter at the plate hit a ball straight to Jim Borden. Jim held out his glove, and caught it in midair.

"Woo-hoo!" Katie shouted out.

The batter and Jim Borden both stopped and stared at her.

"What are you doing here?" the batter asked Katie.

"Mike Reed invited me," Katie explained. "I called the stadium this morning, and he said I could come to practice."

"Oh, all right," the man with the bat said. "But stay out of the way. I've got to get Jim ready for the game today. He's a little out of practice."

Katie looked at him curiously. "Who are you?"

"Joe Tarren," the man with the bat told her. "I'm the team manager."

"Is that the same as a coach?" she asked him.

Joe shook his head. "No. I'm in charge of training the whole team. We do have coaches, but they train different positions. Like we have a pitching coach, and a batting coach."

"I really think you need an infield coach," Katie told Joe.

Joe Tarren stopped smiling. "Oh you do, huh?" he asked, sounding very annoyed. "Are you some sort of baseball expert?"

Joe Tarren was kind of scary. But Katie had

to be brave. She owed it to Mike.

"I'm not an expert," she admitted. "But Mike Reed agrees with me. He told me so on the phone."

Joe looked at Katie. Then he glanced over at the dugout, where Mike was sitting, watching practice.

"Hey, Mike, come here a second," Joe called to him.

Mike jumped up and ran out onto the field. "Hi, Katie," he greeted her.

"You know this kid?" Joe asked Mike.

Mike nodded. "We met at the game yesterday. She's the one who convinced me to keep playing."

"And we all know how that worked out," Joe Tarren groaned.

"It's not all his fault," Katie told the manager. "Mike's new to the game. He needs more practice. And a good teacher."

"Someone like you, Jim," Mike said. He slung an arm over Jim Borden's shoulder. "And

I'm not the only one. All of the guys in the infield could really learn a lot from you."

"Jim Borden would be the perfect infield coach," Katie suggested.

Katie looked hopefully at Joe. So did Mike.

Joe stood there for a moment. He didn't say a word. Katie got really scared. She wasn't sure what he might do.

But then Joe smiled. A big, bright smile.

"What a great idea!" he exclaimed. "I don't know why I didn't think of it." He stopped for a minute. "Is that something you'd be interested in, Jim?"

Jim Borden nodded excitedly. "Would I ever!

I gotta tell you, Joe. I'm getting a little old to be making some of those long throws."

"You know, Jim, I've always been curious about how you made that double play during the World Series five years ago," Mike said. "How did you know that player was heading to third base? He was behind you. It was like you had eyes in the back of your head."

"Oh, that one," Jim remembered. "The trick is to think about what you would do in that exact same situation. Chances are the other player is thinking the same thing . . ."

Katie watched as Mike listened to everything Jim was saying. Katie could tell he was already learning a lot. Joe Tarren looked really happy about that.

Phew. Mike Reed was going to be okay. And Jim Borden would love being an infield coach. That was one big problem solved. Yeah!

Katie left the stadium feeling as though she'd hit a grand slam home run!

GO PORCUPINES!

Chapter 12

Katie was surprised to see so many of her friends hanging around Mrs. Derkman's roses later that afternoon. Emma W., Mandy, Miriam, and Jessica all seemed to be helping Suzanne garden.

Katie watched as Suzanne gently pruned one of the branches from a rosebush. Her best friend was smiling happily under the big brim of her straw hat.

Emma W., Mandy, Miriam, and Jessica didn't look too happy, though. They looked absolutely miserable.

"Miriam, I want you to mix some rotting fish into the soil around the plants," Suzanne barked. "The fish are over there in the fertilizer bin. Emma W., you can help her."

Miriam made a face. "I'm not going anywhere near rotting fish," she said. "That stinks."

"The roses love rotting fish in their soil. Dead fish make great fertilizer," Suzanne insisted.

"But they're gross," Emma complained.

"Nobody said gardening was going to be

pretty," Suzanne told her. "Now go get the fish, soldiers."

Katie cocked her head curiously. Soldiers? That was a weird thing for Suzanne to be calling her friends.

Emma W. and Miriam sighed heavily, but they began to walk over to the fertilizer bin.

"What's going on?" Katie asked in a low voice.

"Suzanne called us all up and asked us if we wanted to help her with the gardening," Emma W. whispered. "She made it sound like it would be fun, so we all came over."

"But it's not fun at all," Miriam added. "Suzanne is so bossy. She keeps saying she's the general and we're her soldiers in some war."

"The War of the Roses," Katie said knowingly.

Emma W. nodded. "That's the one. Who ever heard of a flower war?"

Katie opened her mouth to answer, but before she could say a word, Suzanne started shouting again.

"Mandy, stand back from those babies!" Suzanne shouted. "You're overwatering them."

"We've got to do something," Emma W. told Katie.

"I never thought I'd say this, but I want the old Suzanne back," Miriam said. "The one who practically faints if she gets a speck of dirt on her clothes."

Katie looked over at her best friend. She was all covered in mud and mulch. Her clothes were hideous. And that big straw hat was starting to fray around the edges. That wasn't the funky, cool Suzanne Katie knew and loved at all.

Like Miriam, Katie wanted her old friend back!

"Suzanne, come here, I need to talk to you," Katie called out.

"I can't," Suzanne called back from underneath her straw hat. "I'm on guard."

"But the gardening contest is over," Katie told her. "Mrs. Derkman got third place."

"Don't rub it in," Suzanne growled.

"Come on, Suzanne, just for a minute," Katie said.

"Well, all right," Suzanne agreed. She walked over toward where Katie, Emma W., and Miriam were standing. "But only for one minute. And then we've got to get back to the babies. Right soldiers?" she asked Miriam and Emma W.

Emma W. and Miriam didn't answer.

"Don't you think you're taking this gardening thing too far?" Katie asked her gently.

"What are you talking about?" Suzanne wondered.

"You're not acting or dressing like yourself anymore," Katie pointed out.

"This is what gardeners wear," Suzanne explained. "And I love to garden."

"But you don't have to wear your gardening clothes all the time," Katie said. "Mrs. Derkman doesn't dress that way unless she's working with her roses."

"Her *babies*," Suzanne corrected her.

"Okay, babies," Katie repeated. "The thing is, Suzanne, Mrs. Derkman doesn't just garden. She does other things, too. Like teaching, and traveling. Some nights I hear her singing along with Mr. Derkman while he plays his ukulele in the backyard."

"But gardening is the most important thing in her life," Suzanne insisted.

"Did she say that?" Katie asked.

Suzanne frowned. "Well, no. Not exactly. But those babies need her . . . and they need me, too!"

"No one's saying you have to stop gardening," Katie said. "You just don't have to do it all the time. Don't you miss wearing pretty glittery clothes?"

Suzanne looked down at her dirty fingernails, her faded overall shorts, and her ugly brown-rubber gardening shoes. Then she glanced at her reflection in the window of Mrs. Derkman's car, which was parked outside the house.

"Oh wow. I look awful," she murmured. "I'd

better get home and put on some clean clothes,"
Suzanne said. "And paint my nails with glitter
polish."

"Good idea," Emma W. said.

"And braid my hair," Suzanne continued.

"Cool!" Miriam cheered.

"And maybe buy a new pair of shoes,"
Suzanne added. "These gardening shoes are
awful." She turned and started down the street.

"You're going right now?" Katie asked her.

"There's not a minute to waste," she said.

She smiled at Katie. "Thanks for telling me how awful I looked."

"You're welcome," Katie said with a laugh.

"I can't believe it!" Suzanne exclaimed. "I practically turned into someone else. And in just a few days. That's got to be the fastest switch in history!"

Katie smiled. She knew that wasn't true at all. But she didn't say anything. After all, what *could* she say?

Home-Run Riddles!

Here are some of George and Kadeem's favorite baseball riddles. Use them the next time you and your pals are having a joke-off!!

Why do you need to take a baseball player with you when you go camping?
To pitch the tent!

Where does a catcher sit at the dinner table?
Behind the plate!

What do you get when you cross a baseball player and a tree?
Babe Root!

Why does it get hot after a baseball game?
All the fans go home!

Why did the baseball coach buy a big broom?
He wanted to sweep the World Series!

About the Author

Nancy Krulik is the author of more than 150 books for children and young adults, including three *New York Times* best sellers. She lives in New York City with her husband, composer Daniel Burwasser, and their children, Amanda and Ian. When she's not busy writing the Katie Kazoo, Switcheroo series, Nancy loves swimming, reading, and going to the movies.

About the Illustrators

John & Wendy have illustrated all of the Katie Kazoo books, but when they're not busy drawing Katie and her friends, they like to paint, take photographs, travel, and play music in their rock 'n' roll band. They live and work in Brooklyn, New York.